TESSA KRAILING

The Petsitters Club Winter Special

The Christmas Kitten

Illustrated by Jan Lewis

BARRON'S

First edition for the United States, Canada, and the Philippines published by
Barron's Educational Series, Inc., 1999

First published in Great Britain in 1999 by Scholastic Children's Book,
Commonwealth House, 1-19 New Oxford Street,
London WC1A 1NU, UK

All inquiries should be addressed to:
Barron's Educational Series, Inc.
250 Wireless Boulevard
Hauppauge, New York 11788
http://www.barronseduc.com

ISBN 0-7641-1184-1
Library of Congress Catalog Card No. available on request.

Printed in United States of America
9 8 7 6 5 4 3 2

Chapter 1

Something Special

"Dad," said Sam at breakfast. "What are we going to do for Christmas this year?"

Dad, opening his morning mail, looked puzzled. "Christmas?"

"It's not far away," she reminded him. "Only two weeks."

He shook his head. "Can't say I've thought about it. What did we do last year?"

"Nothing much," said Sam. "Except you bought a real tree, not a plastic one. It looked nice – until the lights stopped working."

"I'll get some new ones." He started reading a letter.

Sam sighed. Sometimes she couldn't help wishing he was more like other people's fathers. Oh, in many ways it was great having a cartoonist for a dad. Lots of laughs. But he was always so busy thinking up good plots for his comic strip that he forgot about things like vacations. Or birthdays. Or Christmas.

She tried again. "But Dad, couldn't we do something special this year?"

"How do you mean – special?" he asked.

"Something … well, different. Like how other people go away to stay with relatives. Or have relatives to stay with them."

He looked bewildered. "But we don't have any relatives other than from Great Aunt Cynthia. And you know she doesn't like traveling in the middle of winter."

In any case, Sam thought, having Aunt Cynthia come for Christmas might be a mixed blessing. She was a wonderful cook but she was very fussy.

"Tell you what," said Dad. "This year we'll buy a nice cake with icing and candles. Then you can ask the other Petsitters over to celebrate."

Sam tried to look pleased, but she suspected that Jovan, Matthew, and Katie would be far too busy with their own families to come. Most other people spent Christmas Day stuffing themselves full of food and opening presents. Last year she and Dad sat at the kitchen table eating turkey burgers, and in the afternoon he went back into his den to work on his comic strip.

She cleared away the breakfast things and took some leftover crusts into the backyard. A robin, perched on the fence, watched her put the crusts on the bird table, his head on one side.

"Sorry, we ran out of bacon," she told him. "Dad's going to buy some today at the supermarket. That's if he remembers." She turned back to the house.

"Hi, Sam," said a voice.

Startled, she swung around. The backyard was empty except for the robin. Surely it couldn't...?

Then she saw a round, cheerful face looking over the fence and recognized Gary Watts, who lived next door. "Oh, hi," she said.

She liked Gary. He always treated her like an equal even though he was much older than she was. Recently he had started work as a reporter on the local newspaper, but he still lived at home with his parents.

"I hoped I might see you," he said. "Fact is, I've got a favor to ask. Do you still belong to that Petsitters Club?"

Sam nodded. "Why, are you going to get a pet?"

"Sort of. Actually it's not for me, it's for my girlfriend." Gary's face flushed almost as red as his hair. "Did you know I have a girlfriend?"

"No, I didn't." Sam tried not to look surprised. Up till now Gary had never shown much interest in girls. He preferred football and motorcycles.

"Her name's Marina," he said. "She

works for the *Echo* like me and we've been hanging out together for several weeks now. She's the most amazing girl I've ever met."

"Oh, good," said Sam, thinking if he didn't hurry up she was going to be late for school.

"So I've been wondering what to give her for Christmas. Then yesterday somebody told me about a kitten that needed a home, and I thought great, that would make a perfect present for Marina."

Sam stared at him. "A kitten?"

"Yeah!" He looked triumphant. "She's crazy about animals. She's got bears and tigers all over her apartment."

For a moment she wasn't sure what he meant. Then she said, "Oh, you mean stuffed animals. But a kitten isn't a stuffed animal, Gary. It's a living creature."

"Exactly." He beamed happily at Sam. "You see, I couldn't afford to give her jewelry or expensive perfume or any of those other things she likes. But a kitten would be something special, don't you think?"

"Very special," Sam agreed. "But Gary, I don't—"

"The trouble is," he went on, "I've got to buy this kitten pretty soon or somebody else might take it. But when Marina comes to my house I don't want her to see it — that'll spoil the surprise. So could you please take care of it for me until Christmas morning?"

"Well, yes," Sam said reluctantly. "I suppose I could. But I don't think—"

"Thanks! I'll pick it up today and bring it to you this evening." His face vanished briefly, then reappeared. "Of course I'll give you money for its food and anything else it needs. Bye, Sam."

This time he vanished for good, leaving Sam staring at the fence.

As soon as she reached the school playground she told Matthew and Jovan what had happened. "I tried to tell him you shouldn't give pets as Christmas presents," she said, "but he wouldn't listen. He's so crazy about his new girlfriend, I think he'd do anything to make her happy."

"What if she doesn't like cats?" said Matthew.

"He says she's crazy about animals," said Sam. "But I think he meant the cuddly-toy kind. You know, teddy bears and pandas and fluffy rabbits."

"That's different from a real live

kitten," said Jovan. "Fluffy toys don't make puddles on the floor."

"Or throw up their food," said Matthew.

"Or tear the sofa to shreds," said Sam.

"Kittens need a lot of looking after," said Jovan. "Especially when you first get them. My dad says Christmas is the worst possible time to introduce a kitten to its new home because there's too much noise and excitement going on."

Jovan's dad was a veterinarian, so he knew what he was talking about. Sam began to feel even more unhappy.

At that moment Katie, Matthew's younger sister, came bouncing up. "Is this a Petsitters meeting?" she demanded. "What are you talking about?"

"Christmas," said her brother. "And how you shouldn't give someone a kitten as a present."

"Of course you shouldn't," Katie agreed. She continued, "Our Grandpa is coming to stay with us for Christmas again this year. How about you, Jo?"

"We're going to some friends of my dad's for our dinner," he said. "They own a restaurant so the food will be fantastic. What are you doing, Sam?"

Sam went pink. "Nothing special," she said. "Except Dad said he might get a cake, so would you all like to come over for cake on Christmas?"

The others looked awkward.

"Yeah … if we can get away," mumbled Matthew.

"Depends how soon we finish eating," said Jovan.

"Grandpa usually does his magic tricks on Christmas afternoon," said Katie.

"It doesn't matter," Sam said quickly.

"The important question is, what am I going to say to Gary when he brings the kitten over tonight?"

"Tell him no," said Matthew. "Say you don't believe in giving kittens away as Christmas presents so you won't help him."

Jovan nodded. "Matthew's right. We shouldn't take petsitting jobs if they're against our principles. You must refuse to do it, Sam."

The bell rang for school.

Katie said, "I've got to go. My class is rehearsing our holiday play." She dashed off across the playground.

Sam, Matthew, and Jovan made their way to their classrooms. For the rest of the day Sam worried about what she should tell Gary when he came over that evening with the kitten.

Chapter 2

Kitten-with-no-Name

But when Gary arrived he appeared to be empty-handed.

"Oh," said Sam. "Didn't you get it?"

Grinning, he unzipped his jacket and took out a tabby kitten with a white chest and paws. "What do you think?" he asked, holding it up for Sam to see. "Will Marina like it?"

Sam was speechless. *If somebody gave me a kitten, she thought, I'd be on cloud nine!* Except that Dad would never let her keep it. Oh, he didn't mind her doing the odd petsitting job at home during the holidays. But if she had a pet of her own he would have to look after it while she was at school, and that would interfere with his work. So no kittens for Sam.

"No," she said.

Gary looked surprised. "You don't think she'll like it?"

"Yes. Er, no. I mean, I don't know," stammered Sam. "I'm sorry, Gary, but I can't do this petsitting job. My dad wouldn't let me."

"Wouldn't let you what?" asked Dad, coming into the hall behind her.

"Gary bought a kitten for his

girlfriend," Sam explained. "He wants me to look after it for him until Christmas morning, but while I'm at school all day you'd have to do the looking after. So I told him I can't."

Dad stroked the kitten's head with a gentle finger. The kitten opened its small pink mouth and mewed faintly. "It's Saturday tomorrow," said Dad. "And next Friday school will be letting out for Christmas. I don't mind looking after it until then if you want to do the job, Sam."

Sam clenched her fists tightly behind her back. "It isn't only that. Us Petsitters think it's cruel to give pets away as presents. A kitten isn't a toy, it's a living creature."

Gary looked bewildered. "Marina isn't cruel. She's very, very soft-hearted. She'll love the kitten, I know she will." He held it up for Sam to admire. "Don't you think it's cute?"

"Mmm, yes." Sam was terribly torn. If she refused to do this petsitting job, what would happen to the kitten? Gary didn't know the first thing about caring for animals. And it looked so tiny and helpless...

"Besides, I've paid for it now. I can't give it back." He put it into her hands. "Please, Sam. I know it will be safe with you until Christmas."

The kitten put two unsteady paws against Sam's chest. It peered into her face with short-sighted blue eyes. She held it gently, stroking its head.

"How old is it?" she asked.

"About eight weeks, I think," Gary said vaguely. "Maybe nine."

Poor little thing, it must be missing its mother. Sam asked, "Is it a boy or a girl?"

Gary shrugged. "No idea."

Dad inspected the kitten's underbelly. "It's a boy."

"Oh, yes," said Gary. "They did tell me when I bought it, but I forgot."

Sam held the kitten closer. "What about his food? And somewhere for him to sleep? And he'll need a litter box."

Gary fished in his pocket and brought out some money. "Will that be enough?"

With her free hand Sam took the money. "Yes ... but there are going to be other things as well."

"Just let me know when you want some more." Gary turned to the door. "Thanks, Sam. I'm really grateful."

"Wait!" Sam followed him to the door.

"You haven't told me the kitten's name."

"It doesn't have a name. I thought I'd leave that for Marina to choose. Bye for now!" With a cheery wave he vanished down the sidewalk.

Sam closed the door and turned to her father. "Honestly!" she exclaimed. "He dumps this poor little kitten on us with no bed, no food, no litter box, no toys, no nothing. And it's too late now to go out and buy anything. What am I supposed to do?"

"If I were you," said Dad, "I'd call Jovan and ask for help. His dad's a veterinarian. He should be able to supply most of the things you need."

"That's a brilliant idea! I'll call him right away." She dropped a reassuring kiss on the kitten's nose. "Don't worry, little one. It's not you I'm mad at, it's that useless Gary. Imagine not even giving you a name!"

The kitten mewed again, as if he agreed with her.

"You'll have to call him something," said Dad. "He can't stay anonymous for the next two weeks."

Sam said doubtfully, "But won't he get confused if we give him a name and then Marina calls him something different?"

"I don't see why. Most of us answer to several names, if you think about it. You call me 'Dad,' Aunt Cynthia calls me 'George,' and my editor calls me 'you lazy hound.'" He grinned. "Which reminds me, I'd better get back to work."

He disappeared into his den.

Sam stared down at the kitten. Surely Marina would fall in love with him at first sight. He was miles better than any cute and cuddly toy. The question was, would she look after him properly?

"We'll worry about that tomorrow," she told the kitten. "Dad's right, though. I'll have to give you a name – but what?"

Still thinking, she went into the kitchen and picked up the telephone. With the kitten in her lap she dialed Jovan's number. His mother answered and gave the phone to Jo.

"I need your help," Sam told him. "I've got an anonymous kitten and I don't know what to do with it."

"A nonny-what?" asked Jovan.

Sam giggled. "A kitten with no name. If I give you a list of things I desperately need could you please bring them over? Your dad should have most of them in his office."

"Yeah, okay. I'll just get something to write with…"

While he was gone Sam smiled at the kitten. "Did you hear that? He called you a nonny-what. Hey, that's not a bad idea! I can't give you a real name, so if I call you Anonymous you can be Nonny for short. What do you think?"

The kitten rested his chin on her arm and closed his eyes.

"Go to sleep, Nonny," she whispered. "Sweet dreams."

Jovan came back to the telephone. "Okay, Sam. Give me the list and I'll get my mom to drive me over with the stuff."

"I thought you were going to refuse this job?" he said when he arrived an hour later. "We agreed you'd say it's against our principles."

"I know," said Sam. "But when I saw Nonny I couldn't do it. Look at him, Jo. He's so small and helpless. Gary would never be able to look after him properly. I know he wouldn't. Did you bring the things I asked for?"

"Yeah." Jovan heaved a large bag onto the kitchen table. "Dad says he should be fed at least three times a day and he'll need plenty of water. Has he been trained to use a litter box yet?"

"I don't know," said Sam. "He's already made two puddles on the kitchen floor, but that could be because he had nowhere else to go."

"With luck he'll already have learned what to do by copying his mother." Jovan unpacked some cans of kitten food, a litter box, and a bag of litter. "Dad says a cardboard box will do for his bed as long as you give him something warm to sleep on, like an old blanket. Oh, and he sent you this booklet, *Caring for Your Kitten.*"

"Thanks, Jo." *But Nonny isn't my kitten,* she thought. *He's Marina's.*

Jovan stared down at the kitten dozing in her lap. "He's going to need an awful lot of looking after. How will you manage when you're at school?"

"Dad says he doesn't mind helping. Anyway, we have off next week."

"Yeah, I know." Jovan sounded depressed.

Sam looked at him curiously. "What's the matter? Aren't you looking forward to Christmas?"

"It's not Christmas I'm worried about," he said. "It's the end of the semester. You know Katie's class is doing a holiday play? Well, her teacher, Mrs. Bennet, sent for me today and asked me if I'd look after the donkey."

"What donkey?"

"Someone's lending them one to be in the play. Mrs. Bennet said she'd heard I know about donkeys and that I belong to the Petsitters Club, so she thought I'd be just the right person." Jovan heaved a troubled sigh.

"But that's great!" said Sam.

"Is it?" Jovan sounded doubtful.

"Yes, because you *do* know about donkeys and you *are* the right person," said Sam. "So now we've both got a petsitting job!"

Chapter 3

A Terrible Shock

"I don't know what you're worried about," Matthew said when he met Jovan in the park next morning. "After all, you were the one who rescued Dillon when he was about to be sold. And you go to visit him a lot at the Donkey Sanctuary. Mrs. Bennet's right, you *are* our donkey expert. So what's the problem, Jo?"

"Dillon's a very old donkey," Jovan reminded him. "He's quiet and easy to handle. But this donkey they're borrowing for the play is probably young and lively and hard to handle."

"Where are they getting it from?" asked Matthew.

"A farmer friend of Mrs. Bennet's. He's going to bring it before the dress rehearsal on Thursday morning and pick it up after the play in the afternoon. I expect I'll be responsible for it all the time it's not actually on stage." Jovan sighed heavily. "It's not going to be easy."

"No petsitting job is ever easy." Matthew glanced at Bruno, the black-and-white mongrel dog he walked regularly for his neighbor Mrs. Wimpole. "Take Bruno. If I don't watch him he starts digging up people's flower beds and then I'm the one who gets the blame. I don't mind telling you, Jo, I get really fed up with this job sometimes."

"Why don't you stop doing it, then?"

"I can't. If I didn't walk him every day Mrs. Wimpole wouldn't be able to keep him. She's too old and not well enough to walk him herself."

"At least Bruno's only small," Jovan pointed out. "Donkeys are a lot, lot bigger. And the worst thing is they're not housebroken. My dad says I'd better take a bucket and a shovel."

Matthew grinned. "And a mop."

"It's no joke," Jovan said gloomily. "If I let this donkey make a mess on the floor Mr. Grantham will be furious!"

The thought of their principal being furious wiped the grin off Matthew's face.

The reputation of the Petsitters Club was at stake here. "I'll help you," he said.

"Will you?" Jovan looked more cheerful. "Thanks, Matt. By the way, you know that kitten Sam wasn't going to look after? Well, when she saw it she changed her mind."

"I was afraid that might happen." Matthew sighed as an impatient Bruno pulled on the leash. "I'd better take him home."

"Yeah, okay. See you at the game this afternoon?"

"Mmm," said Matthew. "Bye, Jo."

For once his mind wasn't on soccer. He was thinking about having to walk Bruno every day. It must be the most *boring* petsitting job ever! He wished he could think of a good reason not to do it anymore.

But when he returned Bruno to Mrs. Wimpole she said, "You're a very kind boy. I don't know how I'd manage without you." Leaning on her cane, she bent awkwardly to pat Bruno's head. Since falling down the stairs some months ago she seemed to find moving around more difficult than ever.

Matthew immediately felt ashamed. "That's all right," he mumbled.

She straightened. "Would you like a fudge brownie?"

"Yes, please!"

She took out a tin from the cabinet and opened it. "I expect you and Katie are looking forward to Christmas?"

"Yes, we are." Matthew helped himself from the tin. Mrs. Wimpole nearly always gave him something to eat when he brought Bruno back. It was her way of rewarding him. "Are you spending Christmas with your son and his family again this year?"

Mrs. Wimpole shook her head. "They're going to Florida for some winter sunshine. But I don't mind. In fact, I'm quite looking forward to staying at home for once. It'll be nice and restful, just me and Bruno."

Matthew's heart sank. That meant he would have to walk Bruno even on Christmas Day!

Mrs. Wimpole replaced the lid on the tin and put it back in the cabinet. "Goodbye, Matthew. And thanks again for being so kind."

"No problem," he muttered, and went next door to his own house.

He found his sister in the kitchen feeding bits of banana to Archie, her pet cockroach. "Katie, you know this holiday play your class is doing," he said. "Are you going to be in it?"

"Yes, I'm a shepherd," she said.

"Don't you mean a shepherdess?"

"No, a shepherd," said Katie. "I've got a moustache and a beard and I have to point at the sky and say, 'Lo, there's a star in the east.' Will you come and watch?"

Matthew grinned. "Wouldn't miss it! Did you know Jo's been asked to look after the donkey."

Katie nodded. "Actually it was me who suggested it to Mrs. Bennet. She says he can be a shepherd, too."

Matthew stared at her. "Jo's got to dress up as a shepherd?"

"Well, he can't be a king because he has to come on leading the donkey," Katie explained. "And when we're in the stable he has to hold the donkey and make sure it doesn't move around too much. So that means he'll have to be a shepherd."

"Are you *sure?*" asked Matthew unbelievingly.

"Positive." Katie peered into her cockroach's box. "What's the matter, Archie? Aren't you hungry?"

Matthew let out a silent whistle. Suddenly he didn't envy Jovan anymore. He'd sooner walk Bruno six times a day than have to dress up as a shepherd!

He said out loud, "I'm sure Jo doesn't know. He thinks he just has to look after the donkey when it's not on stage."

"But the donkey's on stage nearly all the time." Katie took another look into the cockroach's box. "I don't know what's the matter with Archie. He seems to have lost his appetite."

Poor old Jo was in for a terrible shock, Matthew thought. He wondered if he should warn him when they met at the soccer game that afternoon. The trouble was that when Jo found out what was involved he would almost certainly refuse to do the job. And then Mrs. Bennet would ask one of the other Petsitters to be a shepherd instead. Himself, for example...

"Listen, Katie," he said. "If you see Jo don't mention anything about him having to be a shepherd."

Katie looked surprised. "Why not?"

"He might need a bit of persuading. You'd better leave it to me. I'll tell him."

"Oh, all right." said Katie reluctantly, replacing the lid on the cockroach's box. "What's Sam doing this morning? Is she going up to the riding stables?"

"I don't think so," said Matthew, still trying to picture Jovan dressed as a shepherd. "Not now that she's got this petsitting job looking after Gary Watts's girlfriend's kitten."

"So she said yes after all!" Katie jumped up. "I'll go and see if she wants any help."

Chapter 4

Questions About Marina

Sam sat on the kitchen floor, rolling one of Dad's old socks into a ball. "Sorry I haven't got any real toys for you to play with, Nonny. I'm afraid this is the best I can do." She batted the rolled-up sock gently towards the kitten.

Nonny stared at the makeshift ball as if wondering what on earth it could be.

Then he leaped in the air and pounced on it with all four paws at once. Sam watched him, delighted. Last night when he arrived he had looked very lost and frightened, but this morning he seemed much bolder. She batted the sock-ball again and the kitten chased it, skidding a little on the tiled floor.

Sam sighed. "Oh, Nonny. Christmas is going to be bad enough this year without having to hand you over to Marina. I wish I knew more about her…"

The doorbell rang. She picked Nonny up and went to answer it.

It was Katie. "I came to see the kitten," she said. "Oh, isn't he sweet! I'm not surprised you changed your mind about looking after him."

"I didn't have much choice really. Come inside." She led Katie into the kitchen. "Jo gave me a booklet called *Caring for Your Kitten*. It says you should let a new kitten get used to one room at a time, so I thought I'd start with the kitchen. It's warm in here and it doesn't matter too much if he piddles on the floor."

"Does he piddle often?" asked Katie.

"Very often," Sam admitted. "I think he knows what the litter box is *for*, but he keeps forgetting to use it. Do you want to hold him?"

"Yes, please!" Katie took the kitten in her arms and sat down on the floor. "Oh, he's so soft and cuddly. What's he called?"

"Nonny. It's short for Anonymous, because he doesn't have a real name yet."

Katie stroked the kitten's head. "Poor

little thing. I hope Gary's girlfriend is kind to animals."

"I hope so too," said Sam. "In fact, I don't think I should hand Nonny over unless I make sure he's going to a good home."

"How can you do that?" asked Katie.

"Before Christmas comes I'm going to find out everything I can about Marina," Sam explained. "What sort of a person she is, where she lives, if she likes cats, whether she goes out a lot..."

"You mean you're going to spy on her?"

"Not *spy* exactly," said Sam. "More sort of carry out an investigation."

"Like a private detective!" Katie's eyes lit up. "Can I help?"

Sam hesitated. "Well ... yes, you can. Will you stay here and look after Nonny while I go next door to see Gary?"

"If you like. But why do you want to see him?"

"I need to find out Marina's address." She stood up. "If you have any problems Dad's working in his den, but try not to interrupt him if you can help it. He's sort of stuck at the moment and that makes him bad-tempered."

"I won't interrupt him," Katie promised. Nonny wriggled out of her arms and jumped to the floor.

"You can let him wander around as much as he likes in here," Sam said. "But don't let him out of the kitchen."

"I won't." Katie found the sock-ball and started playing with Nonny.

Sam watched him, reluctant to drag herself away. But what she had to do was important. She went out of the back door and closed it behind her.

There was no sign of Gary in the neighboring yard. She'd hoped she might see him by chance and fall into casual conversation over the fence. But no, she would have to go next door and ask his parents if she could speak to him.

Mrs. Watts opened the door. Like her son, she had red hair and a cheerful face. "Hello, Sam. What can I do for you?"

Sam said firmly, "I'd like to speak to Gary, please."

"I'm afraid he's not up yet," said his mother. "He went to a party last night and didn't come home until late. Why do you want to see him?"

"I, er, wanted to talk to him about the kitten."

"Ah yes, the kitten," said Mrs. Watts. "I understand you're looking after it for him. It's not ill, I hope?"

"No, it's fine. But…" Sam decided to be honest. "I really wanted to ask him some questions about Marina."

"Marina?" Mrs. Watts looked surprised. "What do you want to know about her?"

"Just what sort of person she is, really. Like, is she kind to animals?"

"Oh, I should imagine so," said Mrs. Watts. "Gary's brought her home several times and I must say she seems very nice."

"He told me she's the most amazing girl he's ever met," said Sam.

Mrs. Watts laughed. "He never stops talking about her. It's Marina-this and Marina-that all day long. Luckily she seems to feel the same way about Gary."

"Do you know where she lives?" Sam asked.

"I think she has an apartment somewhere off of High Street. But —"

Mrs. Watts broke off as an unkempt figure appeared in the hall behind her. "Ah, here comes the Sleeping Beauty! You can ask him yourself."

Gary's red hair stood on end, his face looked blotchy and pink, his eyes were only half-open. He stood at the foot of the stairs, swaying unsteadily and blinking in the light.

"Gary dear, you have a visitor," said his mother. "It's Samantha from next door. She wants to ask you some questions about Marina."

With difficulty his bleary eyes focused on Sam. "What about Marina?"

"I just wondered...," Sam's courage failed her, "...whether she likes cats?"

"I already told you, she loves all animals," he said.

Mrs. Watts said, "I think Sam wants

to make sure she'll be kind to the kitten, dear."

"Of course she'll be kind to the kitten!" He ran a hand over his unshaven chin. "Excuse me, but I've gotta get dressed. I'm meeting Marina for lunch and this afternoon we're going to the soccer game." He started to close the door.

"Wait a minute," said Sam. "Don't you want to know how the kitten is?"

"Why? Is something wrong with it?" he demanded.

"No, it's fine. But—"

"No problem, then. Goodbye." He closed the door.

Far from satisfied, Sam went back to her own house.

"What happened?" asked Katie when she walked into the kitchen. "Did you find out anything about Marina?"

"Only that his mother thinks she's very nice."

"Didn't you even find out where she lives?" asked Katie.

"She has an apartment somewhere off High Street, that's all." Sam sighed. "He wasn't the least bit interested in Nonny. All he could think about was taking Marina to the soccer game this afternoon." She picked up the kitten and held him close.

Katie said slowly, "Matthew and Jo are going to watch that match. If they see Marina maybe they can find out more about her."

Sam brightened. "That's a brilliant idea! Katie, go home and tell Matthew exactly what I need to know. Then he and Jo can do some detective work while they're watching the game."

Chapter 5

Angelface

"What do you mean – detective work?" asked Jovan.

"Sam wants us to find out as much as we can about this girl Marina," said Matthew. "Like where she lives and whether she's kind to animals, that sort of thing."

Jovan frowned. He didn't want to be

a detective. He had been looking forward to this game all week and all he wanted to do was concentrate on soccer.

"How will we recognize her?" he asked when they reached the soccer field. "We don't know what she looks like."

"She'll be with Gary Watts, that's how," said Matthew.

"I don't even know what Gary Watts looks like."

"Yes you do. He's that short guy with red hair who's a reporter for the *Echo*. He'll be reporting on this game, I expect." Matthew scanned the crowd gathering on the sideline. "As soon as we see him we'll go and stand next to him."

Jovan felt uneasy. It wasn't just this detective business. On the way here he had twice tried to talk to Matthew about helping him look after the donkey for the holiday play, but both times Matthew had changed the subject. He didn't seem to want to discuss it. Did that mean he didn't want to help after all?

He tried again. "I thought maybe we could take turns walking him around the playground."

Matthew looked puzzled. "Who? Gary Watts?"

"No, the donkey! And then when he's on the stage…"

"There he is!" Matthew exclaimed.

"The donkey?" asked Jovan, startled.

"No, Gary Watts!" Matthew pointed towards the penalty area. "He's standing beside a tall, blonde girl. That must be Marina."

Jovan saw a stocky, red-haired young man wearing a leather jacket ... and, beside him, a tall, golden-haired girl with a camera slung around her neck...

"Wow!" breathed Jovan. "She's gorgeous!"

He forgot all about the donkey and the holiday play and Matthew not wanting to help. He even forgot about the soccer game. All he could do was stare at the vision of loveliness that was Gary Watts's girlfriend Marina.

"Come on." Matthew set off across the grass, leaving Jovan to follow at a slow, bemused pace.

While they waited for the game to start the spectators were trying to keep warm by rubbing their hands and restlessly stamping their feet. Matthew took up a position next to Gary Watts. "Hi, Gary," he said.

Gary gave him a puzzled glance. "Sorry, I don't remember...?"

"Matthew White," Matthew supplied helpfully. "I'm a friend of Sam's. And this is Jovan Roy. We're both members of the Petsitters Club."

"Oh ... yeah." Gary frowned. Out of the corner of his mouth he muttered, "Whatever you do, don't mention the kitten in front of Marina."

"In front of who?" Matthew asked, looking blank.

"My girlfriend." Gary jerked his head towards the girl standing beside him. "It's supposed to be a surprise."

Matthew leaned forward. "Hello, Marina. I'm Matthew and this is Jo."

Marina gave them both a dazzling smile. "Hi, boys."

Her eyes were sky-blue, fringed with

long dark lashes. Her golden hair was long and straight and shiny. Jovan thought she was by far the prettiest girl he had ever seen.

The crowd cheered as both teams came out on the field. "Excuse me a sec," said Gary, whipping out a notebook. "I just want to have a quick word with the coach. Won't be long, Angelface."

Marina blew him a kiss. "Missing you already, Chubbychops."

Matthew snorted and dug Jovan in the ribs. Jovan also wanted to laugh, but somehow managed not to. "Chubbychops" suited Gary perfectly, he thought. As perfectly as "Angelface" suited Marina.

When Gary had gone Matthew moved along to fill the space left beside Marina. "Do you like watching soccer?" he asked her.

"Yes, Matthew, I do," she replied. "You see, I love taking action pictures. That's why I asked if I could come with Gary to cover the match. It's a change from doing fashion shows and amateur plays."

Jovan could imagine her at a fashion show. In her short black skirt and red coat she looked as glamorous as any model. Around her neck she wore a gauzy scarf that fluttered in the breeze.

Matthew gave him a nudge. "Ask her if she likes cats," he whispered.

"Why me?" Jovan whispered back.

"Because it's your turn!"

Jovan cleared his throat. He leaned forward to address Marina. "Um, we were just wondering ... do you like taking pictures of cats?"

Marina looked surprised. "I've never been asked. Why, do you have a cat you want me to photograph, Jo?"

"Not exactly." Jovan flushed. "But you do *like* cats?"

"Oh, yes. I love all animals." She smiled at him. "Don't you?"

"He has to," Matthew answered for him. "His dad's a veterinarian."

But that didn't necessarily mean he loved animals, Jovan thought resentfully. He wasn't particularly happy, for example, about the idea of looking after a donkey that might behave badly in the middle of a holiday play.

The home team won the toss. The game started.

"Did you see that?" said Gary Watts as he rejoined Marina and the boys. "Brilliant save!"

"Awesome!" breathed Marina, clicking away with her camera.

Matthew whispered to Jovan, "At least we know she likes cats. Now all we've got to do is find out where she lives…"

The game ended in a tie. As the crowd cheered both teams off the field Gary turned to Marina. "All right, Angelface? Did you get some good pictures?"

"I think so," she said faintly. "Towards the end I was shivering so much I could hardly hold the camera."

Poor Marina looked half-frozen. She had pulled up her coat collar and wrapped the gauzy scarf over her ears. As they started to leave the ground she seemed hardly able to walk.

"Do you have far to go?" asked Jovan, concerned.

"I live at Dean Court," she told him, clinging to Gary's arm for support.

Dean Court was a large apartment building just off of High Street, about a mile from the soccer field. Matthew said, "We're catching the bus. You can come with us if you like."

"No need," said Gary. "I'll give her a ride on my motorcycle."

Matthew and Jovan followed them out of the field. They watched Marina fasten her crash helmet with fingers made clumsy by the cold. She climbed on to the passenger seat of Gary's bike and wrapped her arms around his waist.

"All right, Angelface?" Gary asked over his shoulder.

"Yes, f-f-fine," she said through chattering teeth. Bravely she smiled at Matthew and Jovan. "Goodbye, b-b-boys.

It's been nice m-m-meeting you."

The motorcycle took off with a jerk, almost unseating her. As it drew away from the curb Jovan noticed something lying in the road. He picked it up and stared at it...

Marina's scarf!

"Hey, wait!" he called. "You dropped your..."

"No!" Matthew grabbed his arm. "Keep the scarf. Don't you see, it'll give Sam a wonderful excuse to go and visit her!"

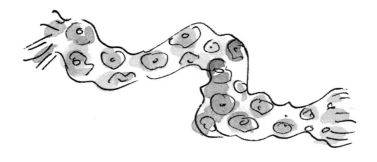

Chapter 6

Marina's Collection

Sam stared at the gauzy scarf, trying to imagine its owner. It smelled of perfume, something sweet and rather exotic, and both Matthew and Jovan had described Marina as being very pretty.

"But what's she like as a *person?*" she asked.

"Very nice," said Matthew.

"Fantastic!" sighed Jovan.

"And she definitely likes cats," Matthew added. "She told us so."

Sam glanced thoughtfully at Nonny. The kitten lay asleep in his box in the kitchen, curled up into a small tabby ball. She still hated the idea of handing him over, even to a very nice, fantastic person who liked cats.

"We also found out she lives at Dean Court," said Jovan. "That big apartment building off of High Street."

Sam frowned. "I don't think Nonny would like living in an apartment."

"I'm sure he'll get used to it," said Matthew.

Jovan nodded. "My dad says cats are very adaptable and can get used to living almost anywhere. And I'm sure Marina will look after him beautifully."

Matthew and Jovan seemed to admire Marina almost as much as Gary did, but could she trust their judgment? It was no use, she wouldn't be happy unless she could see Nonny's new owner for herself.

"When can we take the scarf back?" she asked.

"How about right now?" said Matthew. "It's Sunday afternoon so she should be at home."

Sam tucked the scarf into her jeans pocket. She dropped a kiss onto the sleeping kitten's head and carried his box into her father's den. "Dad, I'm just going to visit Gary's girlfriend Marina. Will you look after Nonny for me, please?"

"Mmm," said Dad without looking up from his drawing board.

She closed the door quietly behind her. "He's still stuck," she whispered. "He's been stuck for three days now. I hope he gets a good idea soon or he'll never remember it's Christmas."

Matthew and Jovan laughed as if they thought she was joking.

But she wasn't.

As they approached Dean Court Sam said, "Won't Marina think it a bit odd, us bringing the scarf here personally? I could easily have given it to Gary."

"She doesn't know you're his next-door neighbor," said Matthew. "We'll just say you're a friend of ours."

"Oh, all right." At the top of the steps she stopped. "What number?"

Matthew and Jovan looked blank.

Sam groaned. "There must be dozens of apartments in this building! We'll never find it if you don't know the number."

They were still staring at each other, wondering what to do next, when a taxi pulled up. The door opened and two long, elegant legs appeared, followed by a short black skirt and a red coat.

"It's Marina!" exclaimed Jovan.

"Boy, that's lucky," muttered Matthew. "She must have been out to lunch."

Sam stared at the tall, blonde girl paying the taxi driver. Marina was certainly very pretty. When she saw them standing at the top of the steps she gave them a friendly smile.

"Hi, boys," she said. "Fancy meeting you again."

Jovan gulped and said nothing. Matthew stammered, "We, we brought your scarf back. You dropped it in the road…" He nudged Sam.

Wordlessly Sam produced the gauzy scarf from her pocket.

"How kind! I was wondering where I'd lost it. Thank you so much." Marina took the scarf and put her key in the lock.

Sam thought quickly. It wasn't enough just seeing Marina, she needed to look inside the place and make sure it was a suitable home for Nonny. As Marina stepped into the hall she asked, "Is it true you've got a lot of stuffed animals?"

Marina looked surprised. "Yes, it is ... but how did you know?"

Sam went pink. Matthew said quickly, "Gary Watts mentioned it. Yesterday. When we were watching the game."

"Oh, did he?" Marina seemed quite satisfied with this explanation. "Great game, wasn't it? I got some terrific pictures of that goalkeeper flying through the air."

But Sam didn't want to hear about soccer. She said firmly, "I'm really, really interested in your stuffed animals. Could we see them, please?"

"In return for bringing back your scarf," Matthew added persuasively.

Marina hesitated, then smiled. "Actually I'm very proud of my collection. Come inside."

As they traveled up two floors in the elevator, Sam could smell that perfume again, as sweet and exotic as Marina herself. She could see why Gary was so crazy about his new girlfriend. Her heart sank at the thought of Christmas morning when she must hand Nonny over to this beautiful, glamorous girl.

Marina showed them into a small,

prettily decorated living room. Sam gasped. There were cuddly toy animals *everywhere!* Cuddly seals and elephants, cuddly pigs and mice, cuddly bears and lions and tigers. And lots and lots of cuddly kittens and cats.

"Oh, wow!" breathed Matthew, staring around the room.

Marina looked pleased. "Do you like them?"

"They – they're amazing!" said Jovan.

Sam cleared her throat. "I notice you've got a lot of cats. Is that because you particularly like them?"

"Oh, yes. I *adore* cats." Marina picked up the nearest fluffy white kitten and clasped it in her arms. "Look, isn't he cute?"

Sam couldn't speak. Her throat had gone dry. She tried to picture Nonny living in Marina's tiny place but found it impossible. With so many stuffed toys around he might get terribly confused.

An awkward silence fell. Jovan broke it by asking gruffly, "Do you have any donkeys?"

"Yes, of course." Marina pointed to a small gray furry donkey on the dresser. "Do you like donkeys, Jo?"

"Well, I *do* like them," he said cautiously. "Actually our school's borrowing a donkey for a holiday play next week and I've got to look after it when it's not on stage."

"A real live one?" Marina sounded impressed. "Perhaps I should come and take some photographs of you for the *Echo*."

Jovan looked first surprised, then pleased. "Yeah, that'd be good. Wouldn't it, Matt?"

Matthew didn't answer. He started edging towards the door. "We'd better go now. Thanks for showing us your collection, Marina."

"Thank *you* for returning my scarf." She saw them out. "Will I see you at next week's game?"

"Yeah, probably," said Matthew, who now seemed in a desperate hurry to get away.

Going down in the elevator Sam was silent, preoccupied with her thoughts. Matthew also seemed preoccupied. Jovan gave him a puzzled look. "I'm sure you can be in the picture as well, Matt," he said. "After all you'll be helping me with the donkey, won't you?"

"Mmm," said Matthew.

* * *

As soon as she got home, Sam went straight into the den. "Hi, Dad," she said. "Is Nonny…?"

She stopped and stared. Dad was no longer sitting at his drawing board. Instead he lay on the floor while Nonny climbed over his chest, chasing a piece of balled-up paper.

"Nonny's fine, as you can see, which is more than I am." Dad struggled to sit up. "How did it go with Marina?"

"Fine," sighed Sam. "She seems really, really nice."

"So now you're satisfied Nonny will be going to a good home?"

"Mmm," said Sam with a heavy heart.

Chapter 7

Matthew's Conscience

By Tuesday, Matthew's conscience was troubling him badly. As he walked Bruno in the park before school he had a silent argument with himself:

You'll have to tell Jo today, said his conscience.

"But if I tell him he'll refuse to do it," said Matthew.

You're his friend. It's your duty to warn him, said his conscience.

"What's the point?" argued Matthew. "He'll find out soon enough."

He'll be furious if he discovers you knew all the time and didn't say anything, argued his conscience. *You MUST warn him!*

Matthew sighed. "Come on, Bruno. We'd better go or I'll be late for school."

When he returned Bruno to Mrs. Wimpole she said, "You don't look happy, Matthew. Is something troubling you?" And when he told her about Jovan and the donkey she said, "Your conscience is right. You must warn him."

At home he found Katie trying to feed Archie, her pet cockroach, who was still not eating. "I'm very worried about him," she said. "Do you think I should take him to see Jo's dad?"

Matthew, deep in thought, didn't answer.

Katie gave him a curious look. "Have you told Jo yet that he's got to dress up?"

Matthew shook his head.

"Honestly, you're hopeless!" Katie said, exasperated. "Well, if you don't do it *I* will..."

"No!" Matthew said hastily. "I'll tell him today, I promise."

The problem was finding the right moment. When they met in the playground before school all Jovan wanted to talk about was Marina. "Do you think she'll come and take a picture of us with the donkey, like she said?" he asked.

Matthew took a deep breath. "Jo, I've got something to tell you—"

"Hello, boys!" Sam raced up to them.

"Whew, I was nearly late. Nonny disappeared and I thought I'd lost him, but it turned out he'd gone to sleep in Dad's shoe."

Matthew tried again. "The thing is, Jo—"

But before he could finish his sentence, the bell rang for school. *I'll tell him at recess*, Matthew promised his conscience.

Recess arrived. But, as they were leaving the classroom, Mrs. Bennet appeared in the corridor. "Ah, Jovan," she said. "Could you come with me, please? I'd like you to try on your costume."

Jovan looked puzzled. "Costume?"

"Yes, your shepherd's outfit." Mrs. Bennet looked him up and down as if trying to guess his measurements. "I've saved the largest one for you so it should be all right."

Jovan stared at her in horrified disbelief. "But — but — but I'm not acting in the play, I'm only looking after the donkey while it's not on the stage."

Mr. Bennet seemed surprised. "The donkey's on stage nearly all the time. I thought you knew that? In the first scene you have to lead it on while the choir sings *Little Donkey*, and in the second scene you have to stand with it in the stable. So you must wear a costume, otherwise you'll look out of place."

"But all the others are little kids!" Jovan protested. "I'll be the tallest person on the stage. Everyone will notice me."

"Not if you bend down and pretend you're old," said Mrs. Bennet impatiently. "Come along, we haven't got much time."

"Wait!" pleaded Jovan. "What about Matthew? He's going to help me look after the donkey. Won't he need a costume as well?"

Mrs. Bennet glanced past him to Matthew, who stood paralyzed in the doorway. "Oh, we won't need two of you on the stage. Besides, I don't have an extra costume. Now hurry up, Jovan, or recess will be over."

As Jovan turned to follow her he cast a reproachful look over his shoulder at Matthew. Matthew felt terrible. He should have said something earlier. Now it was too late.

At the end of recess Jovan appeared in the playground, looking thunderous.

"You knew!" he said accusingly. "You knew all the time I'd have to dress up as a shepherd and go on the stage. That's why you didn't want to talk about it."

Matthew flushed. "I didn't know for *certain...*"

"Yes, you did!" Jovan glared at him. "I've just seen Katie and she said she told you days ago. Why didn't you warn me?"

"I tried, but you wouldn't listen."

"Well, you should have tried a bit harder." Jovan gave an anguished groan. "You should see my costume! It's like a nightgown with a rope tied around the middle. And I've got to wear a kerchief on my head and have a beard stuck on my chin!"

"That's all right, then," Matthew said encouragingly. "No one will ever recognize you in a beard."

"Yes, they will! I'll be by far the tallest person on the stage. Everyone will laugh at me."

"No, they won't," Matthew assured him. "All the moms and dads in the audience will be far too busy looking at their own precious little kids to notice *you*."

"What about Marina? She's coming especially to photograph me and the donkey!" Jovan groaned again. "Oh, *why* didn't you warn me?"

Matthew bit his lip, unable to think of anything to say.

At that moment Sam came over. "Hi, Jo. What did Mrs. Bennet want you for?"

Jovan told her. Sam started to laugh, but then she saw the look on his face and stopped. "Didn't you know you had to dress up?" she asked.

"No, I didn't!" Jovan said bitterly. "Matthew knew, but he didn't tell me. I will never forgive him – never *ever!*" He turned and walked away.

"Is that true?" Sam asked.

Matthew nodded, shamefaced. "I thought if he refused to do it Mrs. Bennet might ask one of the other Petsitters and I was scared it might be me. I feel awful, Sam. What should I do?"

Sam looked worried. "You could try telling him you're sorry."

"I don't think he'd listen to me." Matthew had never felt so miserable in his life. Jovan was his best friend and he hated arguing with him. What if Jo never spoke to him again?

Serves you right, said his conscience.

Chapter 8

A Dry Spell

Sam got home from school to find her father playing hide-and-seek with Nonny.

Surprised, she asked, "Have you finished work already?"

"Never even started," he said gloomily. "It's no use, I haven't had a single good idea for days. At this rate I may as well give up altogether."

"Don't say that." She sat on the floor beside him and lifted Nonny onto her lap. "I'm sure this is just a dry spell. You've had them before."

"They've never lasted as long as this." He sighed. "How was your day at school?"

She made a face. "Matthew and Jo had an argument; now they're not speaking to each other. Dad, I'm scared this might mean the end of the Petsitters Club."

"I wouldn't worry about it. They'll soon get over it."

"I'm not so sure." She set the wriggling kitten back on the floor. "If Jo leaves we won't be able to ask his dad's advice when animals get sick. And if Matthew leaves, Katie will probably go, too. Either way we won't be a real club anymore."

Dad looked sympathetic. "Sounds like you're having a bad day, too."

She watched Nonny whirling around in circles, chasing his own tail. "I'm still not happy about Marina either. Oh, I know she's a nice person, but I just don't feel she can give Nonny the kind of home he needs."

"The trouble is, Sam, it's not your decision," Dad pointed out. "Nonny belongs to Gary and if he wants to give him away as a present that's his business. There's nothing you can do to stop it."

"But Marina's place is so tiny! And she has to go out to work everyday, which means Nonny will be left alone for hours and hours. I don't think Gary's being very sensible."

"Well, as I said before, it's not really your problem." Dad got to his feet. "I'd better get us something to eat. What do you want – pizza or beans on toast?"

"Pizza, please."

When he had left the room she picked up the kitten and held him close. "Oh Nonny, Christmas is supposed to be such a happy time. But it won't be, not this year, what with Matthew and Jo not speaking and Dad being stuck and me having to hand you over to Marina. This is going to be the worst Christmas ever!"

Nonny patted her nose with his paw. Sam blinked away a tear.

"Dad's wrong," she muttered. "It *is* my problem. And there must be *something* I can do about it!"

She put the kitten back in his box, shut the door and went into the hall.

"I won't be long, Dad," she called out. "Just going to see Gary." And she left the house before he had time to ask her why.

By a stroke of luck it was Gary who answered the door. "Hello, Sam. Did you want something?"

"Yes, I need to talk to you," she said firmly. "About the kitten—"

"Ssssh!" He cast a quick glance over his shoulder. "Marina's here."

Sam lowered her voice. "I don't think you should do it, Gary. I mean give her a kitten for Christmas without asking her first. She may not want—"

"Oh, for heaven's sake!" he interrupted. "Of course she'll want it. I keep telling you, she's crazy about animals."

"She may be crazy about *toy* animals," said Sam. "But a real live kitten's different. You have to feed them three times a day and teach them how to use a litter box. Nonny's learning, but he still makes mistakes. And Marina's place is so small and tidy. He could do a lot of damage if he's left alone all day."

Gary looked surprised. "How do you know what Marina's place is like?"

Sam flushed. "Er ... well, I—"

"Who is it?" Marina appeared in the doorway behind him. "Oh, hello, Sam. What are you doing here?"

Sam flushed even deeper. She didn't dare speak.

"She lives next door," Gary explained. "I didn't know you two knew each other."

"We met last Sunday," Marina said. "She came with those two nice boys to return my scarf. I did tell you about it, Chubbychops."

Gary nodded slowly. "Oh ... yeah. But I didn't realize the girl was Sam."

"And I didn't realize she was your next-door neighbor. Aren't you going to ask her in?"

"No," said Gary quickly. "She's in a bit of a hurry – aren't you, Sam?" He glared at her as if willing her to say yes.

Sam sighed. "I'd better go. Dad's cooking some pizza. Bye, Marina."

She fled down the path, but before she could reach the gate Marina called after her, "Tell Jo I'm definitely coming on Thursday to photograph him with the donkey. I've spoken to your principal and he's given me permission."

Sam kept running until she reached the safety of her own path. Whew, that was a close one!

"Sam?" Gary's voice, coming from the bushes that divided their front yards, made her jump. He must have followed her out of the house. "Why did you go to Marina's apartment? You could have given that scarf to me."

"Yes, I know. But..." She decided to be honest. "I wanted to see where Marina lived. I had to find out if it was a suitable home for a kitten."

"Of course it's a suitable home!" He sounded angry and bewildered. "Honestly, I'd never have asked you to look after the wretched kitten if I'd known you'd make such a fuss about it! Look, tomorrow you'd better give it back to me and I'll ask my mom to look after it instead."

"No!" said Sam, horrified. "You can't do that. Suppose Marina sees him?"

"We'll just have to hide it when she comes over. It's only a week until Christmas, anyway."

She felt a smarting sensation at the back of her nose and knew that at any minute she might begin to cry. She hated the idea of losing Nonny before it was time to give him up. A week wasn't long, but at least she'd have him for seven more days.

"I – I'm sorry, Gary," she stammered. "You're right, it isn't my business. Please let me look after Nonny a little while longer."

He glared at her. "Not if you keep trying to make me feel guilty about it."

"I won't anymore, I promise. And I'm sure Marina will love the kitten when she sees him."

Gary hesitated. "Well … all right. But I'll be over early on Christmas morning to pick it up before she arrives."

"Fine," said Sam with a sinking heart.

* * *

The next morning at school she told Jovan, "I saw Marina yesterday. She asked me to tell you she's definitely coming tomorrow to photograph you with the donkey. She's spoken to Mr. Grantham and he's given her permission."

Jovan looked depressed. "That means it's sure to be in the *Echo*. Everyone will see it, including my dad."

"But no one will know who you are," Sam pointed out. "Not if you're all dressed up and wearing a beard."

"They'll know if my name is printed underneath." Jovan groaned. "I'll never forgive Matthew for this as long as I live!"

Chapter 9

Donkey Day

On Thursday morning Jovan woke with the feeling that Something Awful was about to happen. Then he remembered.

This was Donkey Day!

The day he had been dreading. The day of the holiday play. The day he had to dress up as a shepherd and appear on stage with the donkey and be photographed by Marina. He groaned and pulled the blankets over his head.

But it was no use. He had to get up and eat his breakfast and try to behave as if nothing was wrong. "Good luck," said his father as he left the house, adding with a grin, "Don't forget your shovel!"

"Good luck," said his mother as she stopped the car outside the school gates. "Are you sure you don't want me to come and watch?"

"Very sure," said Jovan firmly.

"Oh well, I expect I'll see your picture in the *Echo*." She waved goodbye and drove off.

The first person he met when he walked through the gate was Mrs. Bennet. "Ah, Jovan," she said. "If you meet me in the parking lot at recess I'll introduce you to Donald."

"Donald?" Jovan repeated, puzzled.

"The donkey. My friend Mr. Forbes is bringing him in time for our dress rehearsal. See you later." She walked off in the direction of her classroom.

Jovan saw Matthew on the other side of the playground and made sure to avoid him. The trouble was that he still had to sit next to him in class. Yesterday he had asked their teacher if he could change places but she told him not to be silly. So when the bell rang they both sat down and opened their books without speaking a word. It felt very weird.

"Good luck, Jo," said Sam at recess. "I hope Donald's nice and friendly and does exactly what you tell him to do."

"So do I!" sighed Jovan.

To his relief Donald turned out to be quite a small donkey, with a shaggy gray coat and large dark eyes. He wore a head-collar with a rope attached and stood quietly beside his owner Mr. Forbes.

"So this is our donkey expert?" said Mr. Forbes, smiling at Jovan.

"I'm not exactly an *expert*," Jovan said modestly.

"Oh, I don't think you'll have any problems with Donald," said Mr. Forbes. "I've brought enough hay to keep him quiet while he's on stage. He'll also need a drink from time to time, so I suggest you keep a bucket of water handy."

"Er, what about a shovel?" asked Jovan.

Mr. Forbes roared with laughter. "Smart boy! I can see you know all about donkeys.

You'll find a shovel next to the hay. He's all yours for now." He handed the rope to Jovan.

Mrs. Bennet patted the donkey's head. "Isn't he lovely? He'll look just perfect on stage. You'd better go and change into your costume, Jovan, or you won't be ready in time."

Jovan's heart sank. "Do I have to? Couldn't I stay in these clothes?"

"No, of course not. The reason we have a dress rehearsal is to give you a chance to try out your costume." Mrs. Bennet spotted a figure lurking not far away. "Ah, I see Matthew's come to help. He can take Donald for a walk around the field while you go and change."

Jovan went hot with embarrassment. "I'd rather not ask him…"

But Mrs. Bennet wasn't listening. "Matthew!" she called. "Will you come and take care of the donkey, please?"

Matthew came right over. Without looking at him Jovan thrust the rope into his hands.

"I'll send you a message when we're ready to start," Mrs. Bennet told Matthew. "Come along, Jovan."

With head down he followed her into school.

At the dress rehearsal Donald behaved perfectly. He allowed Jovan to lead him on and off the stage without any trouble. During the stable scene he stood silently munching hay from a bale hidden behind the manger. The children loved him and Jovan didn't need to use the shovel once.

"Told you so," whispered Katie, in her disguise as a shepherd. "I said it would be an easy petsitting job but you didn't believe me."

"The petsitting part is all right," Jovan admitted. "I'm more worried about my beard."

His false beard didn't feel at all safe. Mrs. Bennet had stuck it on with some foul-smelling glue that made him want to sneeze. Or perhaps it was the hay that made him want to sneeze? Either way he felt decidedly sneezy all the time he was on the stage. And this was only the dress rehearsal!

At lunchtime he took off his shepherd's costume and walked Donald around the field. Out of the corner of his eye he saw Matthew coming towards him and put on a scowl.

"I brought you a sandwich." Matthew pushed a cellophane-wrapped packet into his hand. "It's your favorite, tuna-and-mayonnaise."

Jovan wanted to say he wasn't hungry, but he couldn't because he was *starving*. "Thanks," he said grudgingly.

"Do you want me to hold Donald while you eat it?" Matthew offered.

"No, thanks. I can manage." He turned his back and shared the sandwich with Donald. By the time he turned around again Matthew had gone.

Soon after lunch the parents arrived to take their seats in the auditorium. Jovan kept Donald outside until it was time for their first entrance. Then, while the choir sang *Little Donkey*, he led Donald onto the stage. He heard the audience murmur "Aaah!" and "Isn't he sweet!" and realized with relief that they were too busy admiring Donald to notice the rather tall shepherd with the false black beard. Soon he began to relax. Maybe this wasn't such a bad petsitting job after all.

But then he remembered Marina. Had she come? The hall was too dark for him to see exactly who was in the audience. He could just make out the tall figure of Mr. Grantham, their principal, standing at the back ... and beside him someone who looked as if she might have blonde hair. But he couldn't be sure.

Next came the stable scene. Everything went just beautifully. Donald munched hay behind the manger, Katie said her one line of dialogue without making a mistake and so far Jovan had managed not to sneeze. Then it happened.

FLASH!

Jovan jumped, Donald jerked back his head in alarm, and all the actors stopped speaking. What was it? Where did it come from?

FLASH!

This time Jovan saw that it came from the back of the hall where Mr. Grantham stood. From right next to him, in fact. From the person with blonde hair holding a camera...

Marina! So she had come after all ... and now she was taking photographs of the stable scene.

The actors recovered and started speaking again. Jovan bent down, trying to make himself as small as possible. But the camera flashes had clearly upset Donald. From that moment on he stopped being the perfect donkey and began behaving very badly indeed. He tugged at the rope, he kicked the bale of hay, he trod on the hem of Jovan's costume, and he backed into the manger. Jovan fought to keep hold of him, but Donald had had enough. He wanted to leave the stage – RIGHT NOW!

Achoo! The sneeze that Jovan had been struggling to keep under control finally escaped. *Achoo, achoo!* With every sneeze his beard became looser and his kerchief headdress began to slip sideways. *Achoo, achoo, ACHOO!*

For Donald this was the final straw. He panicked completely and charged off the stage, pulling Jovan after him. Moms shrieked, children screamed, and dads laughed nervously as the little donkey careened through the

auditorium, his hooves skidding on the polished floor. With one hand Jovan clung to the rope and with the other he clutched his beard, now attached to his chin only by a whisker.

At last Donald came to a stop, right in front of Mr. Grantham. FLASH! went Marina's camera. FLASH! FLASH!

And that's when it happened…

The moment Jovan had been dreading…

And he didn't even have his shovel with him!

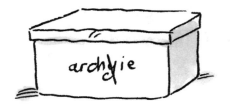

Chapter 10

A Big Black Cloud

"Poor Jo, he looked so embarrassed," Katie told Matthew at home that evening. "Especially when he saw that everyone was laughing. Everyone except Marina, that is. She just went on taking photographs."

Matthew said nothing. He kept his gaze firmly fixed on the TV screen, even though it was a show that he didn't usually watch.

Katie sighed. "I wish you'd stop this stupid quarrel. You're behaving like a couple of spoiled babies."

"It's not my fault," Matthew protested. "I tried to help him. I walked the donkey around the field and I brought him a sandwich. But he still won't speak to me."

"Tomorrow's the last day of school," she reminded him. "If you don't make up real soon you won't see him all during vacation."

"Too bad," Matthew muttered. He turned up the volume to drown out anything else she might say.

Katie stomped out of the room. She hated it when people argued with each other. It was upsetting not only for the two people arguing but for everyone else as well.

The next morning she told Matthew, "I'm still worried about Archie. He stopped hissing and he's not moving around much. I'm going to take him to the veterinarian, after school."

"Yeah, good idea," said Matthew. He still looked annoyed.

"Will you come with me, please? I don't want to go by myself."

He scowled. "Why can't Mom take you?"

"She says she's too busy getting ready for Christmas."

"So am I," he said.

Exasperated, Katie burst out, "No, you're not! You're just afraid you might bump into Jo. But that's silly. You know he hardly ever goes near his father's office if he can help it."

Matthew said obstinately, "Dr. Roy's office is at the back of his house, and if Jo happened to see me there I'd feel really, really embarrassed. Sorry, Katie. You'd better ask Sam to go with you."

Defeated, she went to talk to her sick cockroach. "Poor Archie," she murmured, stroking him gently. "Never mind, my dear. I'm sure Dr. Roy will make you better."

The last day of school was usually a lot of fun. They played games and sang songs and didn't do any real work at all. But this year Katie couldn't really enjoy it. She felt as if a big black cloud hung over her.

She told Sam about it later, when they were on their way to Dr. Roy's office.

To her surprise Sam said she felt exactly the same. "Everyone else keeps saying how excited they are and what a marvelous time they're going to have. But I think my dad's forgotten about Christmas. He hasn't even bought a tree."

"Can't you remind him?" asked Katie.

"I've tried but he doesn't listen." Sam looked depressed. "He hasn't done much work for days. He seems to spend most of his time playing with Nonny. Last night I tried telling him about Jo and the donkey because sometimes he gets ideas from what happens to us Petsitters. But he didn't even laugh. He just said, 'Mmm, very funny' and went on playing with Nonny."

"Jo didn't think it was funny," Katie said. "He was really, really upset about

it – especially having his photograph taken by Marina. Now he's almost certain to be in the *Echo*."

Sam said unhappily, "I'm scared, Katie. What if he and Matthew never speak to each other again? I don't want the Petsitters Club to break up."

"Neither do I," said Katie. She tried to sound more cheerful. "Still, you must feel better about giving up Nonny now that you know Marina's such a nice kind person?"

Sam sighed. "To be honest, I don't feel better at all. But I know he's not my kitten so I don't have any choice."

When they reached the veterinarian's office, the receptionist told them they had come too early. Dr. Roy's afternoon hours didn't begin until five-thirty.

Katie's face fell. "It'll be dark by then. Couldn't he see me now?"

The receptionist looked doubtful. "Is it urgent?"

"*Very* urgent, I think. It's my cockroach, Archie." Katie lifted the lid and held out the box for the receptionist to look inside.

"Wait here," said the receptionist. "I'll have a word with him."

She disappeared through a door into the house.

Two minutes later Dr. Roy came into the waiting room. "Hello, Sam. Hello, Katie," he said. "I hear you've got a sick cockroach?"

Katie showed him the open box. "He's stopped eating and hissing and now he's stopped moving as well. Can you make him better, please?"

Dr. Roy gently prodded the cockroach with his finger. "How long have you had him, Katie?"

"My Grandad gave him to me last Christmas," she told him.

Dr. Roy looked impressed. "So he's a year old? That's a very good age for a cockroach. They don't usually live as long as that."

Katie looked up at him anxiously. "You mean he might die soon?"

Dr. Roy shook his head. "I'm afraid he already has."

She stared into the box. Now that she looked closely she could see that Dr. Roy was right. All that lay among the leaves was the empty body of a dead cockroach. The real Archie had gone.

Sam put an arm around her shoulders. Dr. Roy said, "It's not your fault, Katie.

You looked after him beautifully. No cockroach ever had a better life than Archie. But he was old and tired and it was time for him to go."

Katie began to cry, she couldn't help it. The receptionist fumbled beneath the desk and gave her a handful of paper tissues. Katie wiped her eyes and saw Jovan hovering in the doorway behind his father.

"Archie's dead," she told him.

"I heard," he said sadly. "I'm really sorry, Katie."

Dr. Roy held his hand out for the box. "Would you like me to take care of him for you?"

"No, thank you." Carefully she replaced the lid. "I'll take him home and bury him in the yard."

"I'll help you," said Sam. "Coming, Jo?"

Jovan looked awkward. "I don't think I should."

"In case you meet Matthew, you mean?" Sam gave him a reproachful look. "When are you both going to stop behaving like idiots, Jo?"

Jovan opened his mouth to speak, then shut it again.

"Have you and Matthew had a quarrel?" asked his father.

Jovan nodded shamefacedly, his gaze fixed on the floor.

"So that's why you've been looking so miserable these last few days," said Dr. Roy. "What did you quarrel about?"

"Donkey." Jovan spoke in such a low mumble that only the odd word could be heard. "Shepherd ... beard ... shovel ... photograph."

Dr. Roy looked puzzled. Sam tried to explain, but even when she had finished Dr. Roy still looked puzzled. "Is that all?" he said. "Sounds like a storm in a teacup to me."

"Apologize," mumbled Jovan. He raised his chin and spoke more clearly. "He's got to say he's sorry."

Katie blew her nose on a tissue. "He is sorry, I know he is. If you'd only talk to him…"

"Tomorrow," said Jovan. "At the soccer game. Tell him if he wants to apologize I'll see him there."

Sam heaved an impatient sigh. "Come on, Katie. Let's go."

Katie stuffed the tissues into her pocket. "Goodbye, Dr. Roy," she said, clutching Archie's box tightly.

"Bye, Katie. Bye, Sam." He saw them

both to the door. "I hope Archie's funeral goes well."

"It's going to be the best funeral a cockroach ever had," Katie assured him.

"I'm sure it will," he said.

As the door closed behind them Katie caught a last glimpse of Jovan's face. He looked pretty miserable, she thought. Almost as miserable as she felt herself. Oh, why did Archie have to die now, when it was almost Christmas?

She said to Sam, "You know that big black cloud hanging over us? I think it just got bigger."

Sam shivered. "It feels cold enough for snow. Maybe we're going to have a white Christmas."

Black or white, Katie didn't really care. She just wanted to go home and lay Archie peacefully to rest.

Chapter 11

Peace and Goodwill

On Saturday morning Matthew went next door to take Bruno for his walk.

"You look a bit down in the dumps," said Mrs. Wimpole. "Something wrong?"

Matthew nodded gloomily. "Just about everything. Yesterday Katie's pet cockroach died, so she's upset. And Sam's got to give up the kitten she's been petsitting because it's someone else's Christmas present, so she's upset too. And Jo's upset because I didn't warn him about the donkey business. He says he won't talk to me ever again unless I say I'm sorry."

"And *are* you sorry?" asked Mrs. Wimpole.

"Yes, of course," said Matthew.

"Then this couldn't be a better time to tell him so," she said. "It's Christmas, remember, the time of peace and goodwill."

For the first time Matthew noticed the cards strung out over her mantelshelf, the small tree standing in the corner, the sprigs of holly stuck behind the picture frames. "Don't you mind?" he said curiously.

"Mind what?" asked Mrs. Wimpole.

"Being alone at Christmas. I mean, without your family or anyone."

"You forget, I've got Bruno for company." She patted the dog's head. "We'll be fine, don't worry about us."

Suddenly he felt ashamed of himself for moaning about things going wrong. Mrs. Wimpole hadn't complained once about spending Christmas alone. He said, "I'll tell Jo I'm sorry this afternoon at the soccer game."

"Good." Mrs. Wimpole handed him Bruno's leash. "I hope you're bundled up. It's bitterly cold this morning."

Matthew pulled up the collar of his padded jacket. "Dad reckons it's cold enough for snow."

"Never mind, if you give Bruno a good run you'll soon get warm."

But not even a good run warmed

Matthew up. When he got home he told Katie about Mrs. Wimpole having to spend Christmas on her own. "She says she doesn't mind. But it's not going to be much fun for her, is it?"

Katie said, "It's not going to be much fun for Sam either. She thinks her dad's forgotten about Christmas. He hasn't even bought a tree."

Matthew said slowly, "I suppose we're lucky really. I mean, there'll be five of us, including Grandad. We'll have plenty of company."

"Sam did ask us over for cake on Christmas Day," Katie reminded him. "Do you think we should go?"

"We can't. You know Grandad always does his magic show in the afternoon."

"But he does the same tricks every year," she pointed out. "I wouldn't mind missing them just this once."

Matthew shook his head. "He'd be upset if we went out."

"I suppose he would." Katie sighed. "I thought Christmas was meant to be a happy time for everyone. But it isn't, is it? For some people it's really, really sad."

And Matthew had to agree with her. *Peace and goodwill,* he reminded himself as he set out for the soccer game. But when he arrived at the field there was no sign of Jovan. Had he changed his mind about coming?

"Matthew!" Marina waved to him from the sideline, where she stood with Gary. "Come and join us."

Reluctantly he went to stand beside them.

"Where's Jovan?" she asked. "Isn't he coming?"

"I dunno," muttered Matthew.

Marina pulled up her collar. Today she was wearing a white fleecy coat, boots, gloves, and a woolly scarf. "Are you looking forward to Christmas, Matthew?"

"Sort of," he said.

"Only sort of? I *adore* Christmas! I can't wait to open my presents on Christmas morning." She put her arm through Gary's. "Especially yours, Chubbychops. I wish you'd tell me what it is."

Gary grinned at her teasingly. "If I told you it wouldn't be a surprise. But it's something very special, I promise you, Angelface."

"Oh, I *love* surprises!"

Poor Sam, thought Matthew. She'd love a surprise Christmas present too ... as long as the surprise was Nonny.

But she and Marina couldn't have the same surprise, it wasn't possible.

Suddenly he realized that Jovan had come to stand beside him. "Oh … er, hi," he said awkwardly.

"Hi," said Jovan, staring straight ahead.

Matthew drew a deep breath. "Jo, I'm sorry—" But his apology was drowned out by a roar from the crowd as the teams came onto the field.

Jovan went on staring straight ahead. He obviously hadn't heard.

Matthew drew another breath. "Jo, I'm really, really—"

"Hi, Jo!" Marina interrupted, leaning in front of him. "I was hoping you'd come today. I wanted to tell you I thought you were great on Thursday. The way you held on to that runaway donkey was really brave!"

"Thanks." Jovan cleared his throat. "Will – will my picture be in the *Echo?*"

Marina beamed at him. "Oh yes, definitely. My editor said it was one of the funniest – er, I mean one of the best pictures I've ever taken. He's going to put it in the next edition. You'll be famous, Jo!"

Jovan groaned.

Marina looked surprised. "Aren't you pleased?"

Jovan groaned again, as if he were in pain.

"I don't think he wants to be famous," Matthew explained. "Please could you not put his name under the picture, Marina? Then no one will know it's him."

"I suppose I could ask my editor not to say who it is," said Marina uncertainly.

"But I don't understand. Most people love having their name in the papers."

"Jo's different," Matthew explained. "You see, if he'd known he had to dress up and appear on the stage he'd never have agreed to look after the donkey. It was all my fault for not warning him." He turned to Jovan. "I'm sorry, Jo. I really am."

Jovan grunted something that sounded like "S'all right."

"Why didn't you want to dress up?" asked Marina. "I thought your costume looked fantastic, especially the beard."

"The beard was the worst part," Jovan told her. "The hay in the manger made me sneeze and every time I sneezed the beard got looser and looser."

"I guess you're allergic," she said sympathetically. "I'm like that with cats.

But don't worry, Jo. I'll make sure your name doesn't appear in the paper."

"Thanks, Marina." Jovan looked much, much happier.

The whistle blew and the game started. Gary took out his notebook and Marina focused her camera. But Matthew couldn't concentrate on the soccer. Something Marina had said niggled in his mind. Something about being allergic…

"Cats!" he exclaimed.

The others turned to stare at him.

"Marina's allergic to cats." He turned to Gary. "Did you hear that? She's allergic to CATS!"

Gary glared at him. "No, she's not. She loves cats. She loves all animals."

"Yes, I do," Marina agreed. "But I can't live with them. That's why I collect fluffy toy substitutes. They're lovely to cuddle and they don't make me sneeze."

Gary stammered, "But – but – but – that's impossible!"

"Why?" Marina asked, looking puzzled. "Why is it impossible?"

"Because – because – because it spoils everything!" He sounded really upset.

"I don't understand." Marina turned to Matthew and Jovan. "Why does it spoil everything? What's he talking about?"

Matthew drew a deep breath. "Well, you see, Marina, it's like this…"

Chapter 12

Christmas Surprises

On Christmas Eve Sam sat on the floor, cuddling Nonny. "Tomorrow morning you'll be going to your new home," she told him. "You'll be happy with Marina, I know you will. But oh, how I wish you didn't have to go!" She buried her face against his soft fur.

The front door banged. "Surprise!" Dad called out.

He came into the den carrying a tree. And not a miniature tree either, but a HUGE one, almost as tall as himself. Sam stared at it in amazement.

"I thought you'd forgotten," she said.

"I almost did," he admitted. "It was Matthew and Jovan who reminded me. Oh, and I got some new lights as well. The ones you like; the kind that flash on and off."

He put the box down beside the tree. Nonny wriggled out of Sam's arms and went to inspect it.

Sam looked up at her father. "You've seen Matthew and Jovan?"

"Yes, didn't I tell you? They came over Saturday afternoon, while you were out shopping."

"Oh, Dad!" Sam jumped to her feet. "What did they want? Did they leave a message? Are they friends again?"

"They appeared to be the best of friends. And no, there wasn't any message. It was me they came to see."

"What about?" asked Sam.

"Well, it's sort of a secret." Dad grinned at her. "Don't worry, you'll find out eventually. Now, if I fetch that box of tinsel and stuff down from the loft you can start decorating the tree." He disappeared.

"Why is he being so mysterious?" she whispered to Nonny. "Oh, I wish I'd been here when Matthew and Jovan came. I only went out to buy Dad's present." She sighed. "I wonder if he's got one for me. He might not have had time if he just started to remember Christmas *now*!"

Dad returned with the box of decorations and together they began to decorate the tree. Nonny tried to help them, but only succeeded in decorating himself. Twice he got so tied up in tinsel that he had to be disentangled. Sam told him sternly, "If you're not careful you'll end up on the top branch instead of the angel!"

At last they were ready to switch on the lights. Nonny stared at them, fascinated, as they flashed red and yellow and green. Suddenly he jumped up and tried to catch them with his paw. Giggling, Sam held him safely until Dad switched the lights off again.

When it was time for bed she crept upstairs with Nonny clinging to her shoulder. Usually he slept in his box in the kitchen, but tonight she couldn't bear to leave him. As soon as she set him down on the quilt he curled himself into a ball and closed his eyes, worn out after all the excitement.

"This is our last time together," she told him sadly. "Tomorrow you'll belong to Marina."

She got undressed and switched off the light before drawing back the curtains. No sign of snow yet: the sky was dark blue, clear, and starry. It didn't feel at all like Christmas Eve. For the first time ever she wasn't looking forward to tomorrow.

She climbed into bed beside the sleeping kitten and dropped a kiss on the top of his head. "Goodnight, Nonny. Sweet dreams."

* * *

The next morning at breakfast she gave Dad his present – a red woolen scarf and gloves to match. "Merry Christmas!" she said, and looked around for hers.

"You'll have to wait a little longer," he said. "I can't give it to you yet."

"Oh, *Dad!*" she wailed. "Gary will be here to collect Nonny any minute."

"Yes, I know," said Dad, as if it wasn't anything important.

Puzzled and a little cross, Sam started to prepare their Christmas dinner – a small turkey breast joint, just right for two people, frozen roast potatoes, peas, and carrots. With his head on one side Nonny watched her put the turkey in the oven.

"If you're good I'll give you some," she told him – and then remembered that by dinnertime he'd be gone. Tears came into her eyes. She sat on the floor beside him, picked him up and cried into his fur.

The doorbell rang. Sam froze. "That'll be Gary," she whispered, hastily wiping her eyes.

Dad answered the door. She heard his voice in the hall, joined by Gary's and Marina's. They all sounded very cheerful, laughing and wishing each other a merry Christmas.

"Here she is," said Dad, coming into the kitchen. "Here they both are!"

"Hi, Sam," said Gary, beaming at her.

"Merry Christmas, Sam!" said Marina. "Oh, what a sweet little kitten!"

Speechless, Sam held Nonny towards her. This was the moment she had been dreading for two whole weeks. At last it had arrived.

But to her surprise Marina shook her head. "Sorry," she said. "I'll have to admire him from a distance. You see, cats make me sneeze."

Sam stared at her. "Sneeze?"

"Yes, I'm allergic to them," said Marina. "That's why I collect fluffy toys."

Gary said quickly, "I didn't know until Saturday, when we got talking to Matthew and Jovan at the soccer game. It was when Jovan said that hay made him sneeze—"

"And I told him that cats made *me* sneeze," said Marina.

"And that's how we found out." Gary smiled fondly at Marina and she smiled fondly back.

Sam still couldn't believe it. "You mean Matthew and Jovan have known since Saturday?" She swung around to look at

her father. "So *that's* why they came over to see you! Oh, Dad – why didn't you tell me?"

He looked a little uncomfortable. "I wanted it to be a surprise. Oh, I know you don't believe in giving real live creatures as presents, but Nonny's your kitten now, Sam. You can keep him forever."

"Oh, *Dad!*" She jumped up to give him a hug, taking care not to squash Nonny between them. Dad laughed and patted the kitten's head.

"We have to go," said Gary, guiding Marina to the door. "Come on, Angelface."

Marina glanced wistfully back at Nonny. "He really is a lovely kitten." She turned to Gary. "But I *adore* the gorgeous cuddly tiger you gave me instead,

Chubbychops. Bye, Sam. Have a happy day."

"I will!" Sam promised. When they had gone she told her father, "I'm glad you didn't tell me before. That was the most wonderful surprise I've ever had in my life!"

He grinned at her. "The surprises aren't over yet. There's more to come."

To find out what they were she had to wait until later that afternoon, when Matthew, Jovan, and Katie arrived. "Merry Christmas," said Jovan when she answered the door. "We've come for cake."

"And we've brought our grandad," said Matthew. "He's come to do his magic tricks."

A tall man with a beard stepped into the hall, carrying a large wooden box.

"These are my props," he said. "Where would you like me to do the show?"

Sam took them all into the living room, where Nonny was busy playing with some silver tinsel he had managed to pull off the tree.

"I bet you were happy when you heard about cats making Marina sneeze!" said Jovan.

Sam nodded. "It was the best news I've ever had. In fact, this is the best Christmas I've ever had!"

"We're having a good one too," said Matthew. "Mom and Dad asked Mrs. Wimpole to join us for lunch so there were six of us. Seven including Bruno."

"And look what Grandad gave me!" Katie lifted the lid of a cardboard box.

Sam peered inside. "It's another cockroach!"

"I'm going to call him Archie Two." Katie closed the lid. "He doesn't hiss quite as loud as Archie One, but then he's still young."

"Surprise!" Dad came in carrying a cake with white icing and red candles, all aglow.

"Oh, Dad, you remembered!" said Sam.

"Of course I remembered." He winked at Matthew and Jovan. "All right, let's have some cake and then we'll watch the magic show."

Later, when everyone else had gone, Sam sat on the floor nursing a sleeping kitten. "Dad," she said curiously, "you seem a lot happier all of a sudden. Is that because it's Christmas or have you had an idea?"

"Both," he said. "Yesterday I noticed

something that had been right under my nose all the time."

"What?" asked Sam, intrigued.

"When I couldn't work Nonny did so many things that made me laugh. Then suddenly it hit me. Of course! The adventures of an anonymous kitten. What do you think?"

"I think..." Sam said slowly, "it could be very good."

"So do I." He tickled Nonny behind his ears. "You'll have to decide what you're going to call him, Sam. He can't go on being anonymous now that he's rightfully yours."

She thought hard for a moment, then shook her head. "It's too late to start calling him something different. I'd get confused and so would he." She stroked the kitten's warm body and felt it thrum with a loud, contented purring. "He's Nonny now, forever and ever."

Dad got up and went to open the curtains. "Well, look at that!" he exclaimed. "It's started to snow."

"Perfect," Sam sighed happily.

The End

Join the Petsitters Club for *more* animal adventure!

1. Jilly the Kid
2. The Cat Burglar
3. Donkey Rescue
4. Snake Alarm!
5. Scruncher Goes Wandering
6. Trixie and the Cyber Pet
7. Oscar the Fancy Rat
8. Where's Iggy?
9. Pony Trouble
10. The Rude Parrot

Vacation Special: Monkey Puzzle